Mrs. George Cupples

My Pretty Scrap-book

Or, Picture Pages and Pleasant Stories for Little Readers

Mrs. George Cupples

My Pretty Scrap-book
Or, Picture Pages and Pleasant Stories for Little Readers

ISBN/EAN: 9783744750189

Printed in Europe, USA, Canada, Australia, Japan

Cover: Foto ©Andreas Hilbeck / pixelio.de

More available books at **www.hansebooks.com**

MY PRETTY SCRAP-BOOK;

OR,

PICTURE PAGES AND PLEASANT STORIES FOR LITTLE READERS.

BY

Mrs. GEORGE CUPPLES,

AUTHOR OF "BERTHA MARCHMONT," "THE STORY OF OUR DOLL," "GRANDPAPA'S PRESENTS," ETC.

LONDON:
T. NELSON AND SONS, PATERNOSTER ROW;
EDINBURGH; AND NEW YORK.

1874.

Contents.

CONTENTS.

CONTENTS.

MY PRETTY SCRAP-BOOK.

IT is Dick's birth-day, and his mamma has very
wisely bought "My Pretty Scrap-Book" for him
as a present. Should you like to see what is in
it? Very well, then; stand by my side while I
turn over the leaves carefully.

Ha! ha! ha! do wait till I hold my sides!
What a funny fellow! Are they pulling out his
teeth, or his tongue? It is a shame to tickle his
poor nose all the time, and to play such pranks
with his fine wig. But he is watching, slyly, to
catch one between his finger and thumb.

Oh, how naughty of Judy, to take advantage of
her mistress being asleep. She is trying on some
of Miss Eva's fine clothes ; and see, she has found
her best fan, and as it has a neat little looking-
glass in the handle, she can see her black face in
it. What a start she would get if her mistress
were to open her eyes suddenly ! But cunning
Judy knows that as long as the heat is so great,
Miss Eva will sleep on ; that is to say, if a mos-
quito do not alight on her cheek.

HERE is a scene in our own country,—a little
girl gleaning. It is a very warm day, too; but no
doubt her parents are poor, and she is forced to
work, no matter how warm it is. She must be well
known to the reapers; for few people are allowed
to glean till after the corn has been all housed.

No wonder they are in a hurry. The rain is coming down very fast; and the clouds are so black, they are afraid there may be thunder. I rather think they must have heard one distant peal already, they look so frightened—especially the boy. Theirs is certainly a very funny umbrella; but not a bad way to do if you are caught in a shower, and wish to save your fine feathers, if you have any. Perhaps the little boy has put his cap into his pocket, because he hasn't got one on his head. But I can't help wishing he had been on the outside, so that his sister might have been more sheltered. He should have been more polite.

You will be thinking already that I have a variety of pictures in my Scrap-Book; and so I have. Here is one of a ship in the Bay of Biscay. It is a fine ship, and it is doing its best to make its way through the heavy sea. I fear there has been a wreck, for you see there is a piece of a mast standing out of the water, and a barrel and a hen-coop floating beside it. If the people see it from the ship, it must make them shudder.

" RIDE a cock-horse to Banbury Cross."   The idea
of a king being afraid ! Just look at him !   Would
you be afraid if you had a rocking-horse like this,
with such a splendid tail, too ?   No, of course
not.   A king ought never to be frightened at anything, especially when he has his crown on, and
his pig-tail tied up so nicely.   The horse seems
to be quite ashamed of him.

I HAVE put this picture in that you may make a
drawing of it.   It would be a nice present to
give to mamma, you know, especially if you
coloured it.   If you do, I hope you will be par-
ticular with the cow, she is such a sleek, pretty,
dun-coloured one.

(446)

OUT at the sea-side! Here are two young folk out on the rocks looking for shells and sea-weeds. The girl must be lame, for you can see she has a crutch with her. That must be her brother; and I feel sure she loves him very much indeed, for see how she is laying her hand on his head. I am certain he helps her very tenderly over the rough and wet places; very likely he carries her on his back. I do hope they notice that the tide is rising, because it would be a sad thing for them to be caught by the water. They do look rather sleepy about it, and are too intent upon watching a funny crab.

"Up in a balloon, boys, up in a balloon!"   Well,
I don't think it has been the donkey's fault that
he is here; and he looks very much as if he were
saying, "I'm quite willing to gallop along, but I
should just very much like to know where I'm to
gallop to; and as for the clouds, no doubt they
are very pretty in their way, but how can I eat
them?   I'd much rather have an old stunted
thistle—I really should indeed."   It would serve
the rider right if the donkey were to jump out of
the balloon.   I don't think he'd be so merry then
with his "Gee up, Teddy!"

Now, I do call this a pretty picture. Here is an honest farmer's-man. He has come home from his hard day's work in the fields; and, after his supper, he takes his seat by the door to play with his baby.

HERE is a picture of a lake among the mountains,
and a very pretty place it seems to be. How
nice it would be to have a sail in that little boat!
The wind is sending it along in fine style. I
think you would rather be there than among the
people who are toiling up the steep mountain-path
with the baskets on their backs. Yet I must
say the girls seem content and happy, even
though their work is hard and humble.

AH, here is a generous fellow. That is what you do, isn't it, when anything nice has been given to you? What large pieces he is cutting off, too! I hope he will have enough of cake left to go over them all and leave a portion for himself. No wonder his companions are waving their caps and shouting "Hurrah!"

THEY have got a pretty pair of pigeons in that
basket, I feel certain. Mary is taking very great
care of the cage, holding it as firmly as she pos-
sibly can till Henry gets down from among the
rafters of the shed.

WHAT funny animals! Yes; they are kangaroos.
Do you notice that their fore feet are much shorter
than their hind ones? Poor things, they cannot
run like the dog. And yet they are not to be
pitied exactly, because they can jump ever so far,
and by this means they get along at a great
speed. The mamma kangaroo has a pouch, and
she puts her little young one into it, and jumps
away with it hidden quite snugly.

HERE is rather a sad picture. Two poor men have been wrecked on a desert island. They have managed, however, to put up a tent, and to hoist an old tattered flag for a signal to passing vessels. They have certainly been making the most of it, and trying to be as content as possible; but when they were least expecting it, a sly fox comes stealing along and runs off with the only chicken they were able to save. It is really too bad of Reynard, for he might have been content with the sea-birds. Oh, but look! one of the men is getting ready his gun, and I rather think that the sly fox will be shot.

WHAT lovely ripe grapes! These young folk are carrying them away to make wine of them. It is rather a pity to think the great presses will squeeze them into a mash; but then we couldn't get any wine to drink if they weren't squeezed. The girls don't seem to be eating any of them; but perhaps they have been told not to do so.

HERE has been a wreck in real earnest; but the crew seem to have been all saved by the gallant life-boat. One might think, to look at the heaving sea, that the poor boat would never be able to reach the ship. The man on board is doing his best to direct them, by pointing out how to steer; and he has a rope ready to fling to them.

Now, did you ever see such a sulky face? It is quite shocking! I think we ought to call him Master Crosspatch. He surely must be the very husband of Crosspatch, to whom we say, "Draw the latch, sit at your door and spin;" and whom we advise to "Take a cup, and drink it up, and call your neighbours in!" If poor Crosspatch's husband is like this, perhaps that is why she cannot be so kind as she would like, and why her temper has been soured; for I am sure such a face is quite enough to turn the sweetest cream into a curd.

Oh, how pretty and how cool the water is! The dog is thinking so, at any rate, and is cooling his hot tongue in the clear stream. He would like to get into it altogether, I daresay, but it is not deep enough. His mistress is pouring all the water out again; perhaps because she fancies her dog's tongue has dirtied it. Well, it certainly would have been better if he had gone to the other side; only he couldn't know, being a dog.

How do you like this picture? These girls seem
to be enjoying themselves very much indeed. Not
all of them, though; for poor Miss Dollie is sitting
all alone, no one taking any notice of her, and so
she feels very lonely indeed. Poor Dollie! what
does she care for the fine new·fairy-tale book, or
the story Clara is reading aloud?

THIS is a falcon, and he seems to be a very tame one. That is the falconer's little daughter, and she is talking to the great bird. He appears to be listening very attentively to what she is saying. What can she be saying? Perhaps she is asking him not to touch any of her pet birds; because she has ever so many robins and wrens and finches she likes to feed every morning; and she is asking the falcon not to do them any harm. I don't think she has much to fear; he seems to be such a good-natured bird. I only hope the boys in the village will be half as kind.

OH, fie, fie for shame, Miss Meddlesome Matty! We all know *you* the moment we see you; and we know about how you "lift the tea-pot lid, to peep at what is in it," the moment your grandmother turns her back. Ah! you often get into disgrace with your naughty tricks.

ARE you fond of gardening? If so, you will like to see this picture in my Scrap-Book. See how very industrious the little girl and boy are; and how attentive they are to the wants of the flowers, watering them after the sun is down.

OH dear! what is this? A poor man has been
bathing, and here is a great shark trying to
swallow him. Oh, what a good thing his companions were close at hand, and that they are so
brave! See! one of them is striking his long
spear right into the shark's back; while another
has got hold of their poor ship-mate, and is drag-
ging him out of the shark's very mouth! The
man must be very much hurt. If he has any
children, how sorry they will be to hear of it.

Ah! I thought you would all like to see this.
Here is a whole doll-village, church and all.
Perhaps the boys don't care about seeing it; but
then we must always be polite, and put in pictures to suit the girls. Well, I am sure the dolls
who own all these fine houses must be very
happy dolls indeed; and the little girl who owns
the dolls, and, of course, the houses and the trees
and the church into the bargain, must be the
very happiest little girl in the world. She surely
never cries, and is always good, and is a pattern
to all her friends. Shouldn't you like to know
her, and be invited, along with your own dolls,
to pay her a visit?

I SUPPOSE the boys will like this one better. Here is the king once more, so glad to find himself on a chair instead of on horseback. He is telling the master of the doll-house all about it, and of how nobly he rode the animal, though it tried its best to throw him off. Oh, what a sly fellow! when we know what a coward he really is. The doll, who is the master of the doll-house, seems to be listening most attentively, and is glad to hear that the king has made such a lucky escape.

HERE is the picture of a Highland soldier.   He
is bidding farewell to his wife and little baby,
because he is going away to the wars.   No wonder
his wife is sorry, for she may never see him again.

HERE is a picture of a little girl whose mother is
a widow. She is looking round at the other
children, and longing to be allowed to join them
in their sports; but her mother is so sad that she
can think of nothing else but her sorrow. Poor
little orphan girl.

HERE are a pair of parrots. They are out in the
woods in their native state, and how they do
screech and chatter. One has a green breast,
with a mottled green and black back, with lovely
blue feathers in its wings, and two long red ones
in its tail; the other has a red breast and a red
head, and, though very different, is quite as
pretty. Of course, when they are at home in
the woods, they cannot say, "Pretty Polly," or
speak at all; it is only when they are caught
and tamed that they become so clever. Only, I
think they like being wild best. They can search
for the food they like, and are free as the air.

HERE is a picture of mamma and baby. Mamma
is sitting in the arbour.   Baby is sound asleep ;
which is a good thing, for mamma can now rest
and sit quietly thinking about what she should
do for her little darling.

HERE is a picture of two pearl-fishers. They are offering some pearls for sale to an officer; but perhaps he is too poor to buy them, or he does not require such fine things, because he seems to be refusing to have them.

THIS is Mrs. Taffy, and it is plain she has just heard that her son has stolen the leg of beef. Oh, how stern she does look, to be sure! Taffy will surely never be so foolish and naughty again, and will turn his eyes away the moment he sees a leg of beef or a marrow bone. I know, if my mother looked like that at me, I should be ready to sink down with terror and dismay.

OH, what a lovely Christmas tree! Do not you
wish you were of the company? or that Christmas would bring you just such another? How
it must sparkle and shine with so many candles
and coloured balls! This tree is in Germany;
and do you notice all the toys and pretty presents?

HERE is a little boat, or a canoe rather, shooting
the rapids. The people don't seem to be the least
afraid; for, see! there is a man in the front
waving his handkerchief to some of their friends
on the shore. The men behind are looking a
little anxious, I think,—and well they may.

THIS place is called Funchal, in the island of
Madeira. When you are older you will read
all about it. Those high peaks you see are the
tops of very high hills. They sometimes open and
throw up fire and smoke and rocks and ashes.
The people are not afraid to live here for all that,
and have some of their houses built on the very
rocks which have been thrown up! The people
make wine here, and the ships take it away.

HERE is a terrible sight! A gentleman has been walking among some steep mountains, and has fallen over the rocks, and lies quite insensible.

I THINK this is a very pretty picture. Here is
little Mary in her garden, taking a walk among
her flowers. The gay painted butterflies like to
go there, because Mary has so many sweet flowers.
They like to flutter from one to another; indeed, they need not go to any other, for here
they are sure to find all they could wish. But
then a butterfly is so idle and likes to roam, and
flits away from Mary's garden out into the common and the fields, and here, there, and every-
where. The busy bees are more sensible: they
keep to the roses and the honeysuckle; and as
for the sweet-peas, there never were such sweet-
peas as little Mary's.

On, do look at this picture in my Scrap-Book—
such fun! It is market-day, and all the show-
men have arrived. All sorts of wonderful sights
are to be seen inside if you will but walk in.
"A fat woman!" "a learned pig!" and "a giant
with a tail!" And if you could only hear the
music, it would nearly make you deaf. Bang,
bang, bang, goes the drum at both ends. He
must be a great musician, for he is playing on
another instrument at the same time.

SUCH a gathering of canoes ! It must be a great battle that is going to take place ! All the fighting-men are ready with their bows and spears; while their chiefs are standing up in each canoe, telling them how they are to fight. No doubt the enemy is making ready too; and they will indeed require to be careful, for here is the king himself, in the largest canoe, sitting on a chair of state. He is a very big man, and has his club ready.

An accident has happened to this poor woman's husband. He must have fallen from the rocks, like the traveller we saw. See! that is his poor mother looking out of the window.

OH! here is a loving little pair! We like to see this, don't we? Little Kate and Maggie love each other dearly. They know that the "birds in their little nests agree," and of course that it would be quite shameful if they were not even more loving than the birds. Maggie must be saying,—"Oh! I do love you, my dear, good Kate;" and Kate is saying,—"And I love you, Maggie, you kind little dear." How they would look if we were to tell them that ever so many little boys and girls we know quarrel and fight; and instead of kissing each other, scratch and push each other down! They would scarcely believe us. They would think we were joking, and wanted to make fun of them.

OF course you know the rhyme about the cat
and the fiddle; and how the cow took such a
wonderful jump, and went clean over the moon;
and how the dog was so amused to see the
fine sport; and the dish it ran after the spoon.
But look here! The little dog was quicker than
the dish; for he has got the spoon himself, and
seems as if he meant to keep it. He is telling
Miss Pussy that of course such a fine gentleman
cannot be expected to do without a spoon when
he has his fine coat on.

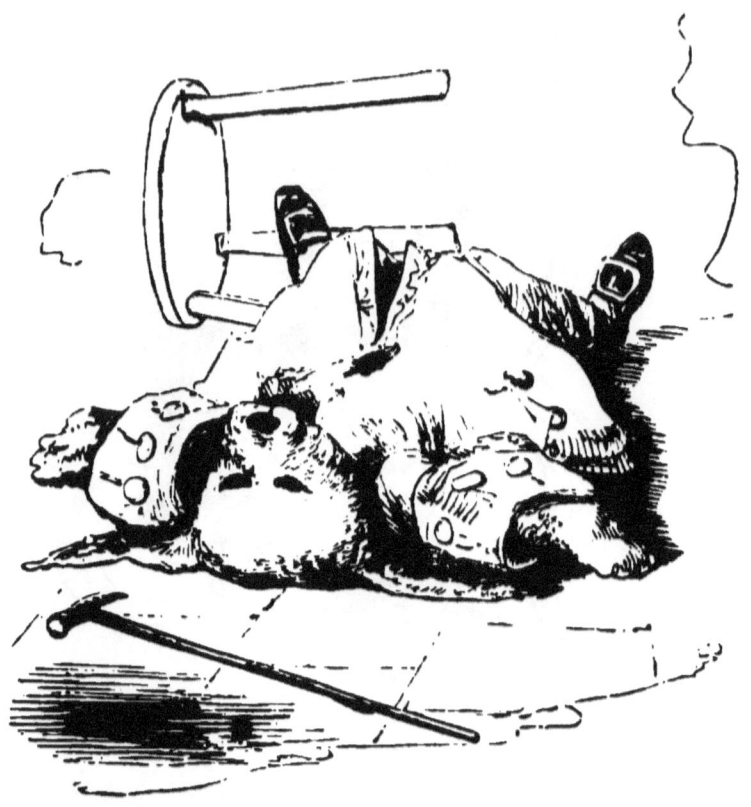

OH! now isn't this too bad? Miss Puss is such
a cunning creature! She had a fancy for the
spoon herself; and when the little dog was busy
telling her how cleverly he had stolen the spoon
from the dish, what did she do but give the little
dog a great push, when down he fell off his stool,
and away she scampered with the spoon herself!
Oh! what a cunning, naughty cat! She had
better run fast; for the dog has caught sight of
his mistress' stick, and will be after her directly.

" WHAT is the matter?" Ah! here comes Miss
Mabel's papa to inquire the cause of the angry
words. Nurse has been nearly driven stupid, and
does not know what to do; for her young mistress has pulled the clothes they were packing out
of the box, and will not allow her to touch them.

THIS is a very different picture indeed. This must be a very gentle girl; for see how all the pigeons and poultry of all kinds are flocking around her to get their breakfast.

You would laugh if you knew why these black
savages are looking so surprised. It is at sight
of the white men! They never had seen such
people before. Some of their friends had, and
had got pieces of cloth from them, which they
are wearing now; but this company had never seen
a white man. They are holding out their hands
to them, and showing by signs that they are glad
to see them. The white men are missionaries,
sent from this country to tell them about God
sending his Son into the world to die for sinners.

I REALLY think this is a very unsafe place to
be in; but Dick Hardy is a very daring boy
indeed, and he is trying to get at the sea-birds'
nests, and quite forgets that he may fall.

Oh dear, what a sad sight! Though I can't say I like rats, I do hope this one will escape, it seems so brave. I rather fear it will never be able to get away, for if it escape from the strong bill of the bird, puss is ready with her paw to pounce upon it.

HERE is a group of Chinese; and don't they look funny? Did you ever see a more comical-looking figure than that little Chinese boy? It is a pity he can't turn his head round to let us see if he has a long queue, or pig-tail, as the long plaited hair behind is called. And isn't it strange to see the woman carrying her baby in a sack on her back, and smoking a pipe like a man—with a staff in her hand, too? That must be the father sitting beside the little boy; and a very fine pig-tail he has of his own. The lady is feeling rather hungry, and so she has brought out her dish of rice. She has no spoon, but uses a little stick instead.

THIS must be Dame Hubbard; and though she has got her cloak and hat off, and is in her own room, she does not look particularly at rest or happy. What can the naughty dog be doing now? Really it is too bad of him to give his kind mistress no peace. See how she seems to be straining her ears to listen if he is quiet and asleep in his cozy basket.

AH! no wonder Dame Hubbard got a start. Here is her naughty dog turning round her spinning-wheel. He seems delighted to see it turn round, and to hear its pleasant whirr; but I am afraid he will be causing some sad mischief to the fine flax his mistress is spinning. He ought to be punished, for the good dame takes such care of him. Just look at the splendid coat she made him, and the fine shoes she bought at the market.

How should you like to
live up here? If you
like snow you would
have it in plenty. This
is a portion of the Alps.
On their heights snow
is always to be found.
But where they approach
the open, level country,
which is much warmer, they are often crowned
with large forests. Vast masses of ice and snow
often separate from the mountains, and rolling
down, overturn everything in their course, and
sometimes cause great loss of life.

HERE is a very sad picture.   A poor man has
been sent to carry home a large hamper; but he
has lost his way, and, having fallen down with
fatigue, he has dropped asleep.   His faithful dog is
watching him; but the snow will soon cover him.
Oh, here comes a man on horseback to his rescue.

AH! here is little baby in her cradle. She has just awaked out of her forenoon sleep, and she thought at first she was all alone, and began to be afraid; but sister Mary was not far off, and hearing the gentle rustle and the half sob, hastened forward just in time to stop the tears from coming. "And was baby frightened?" That is what she would be sure to say. And baby would laugh, and because she can't say a single word yet, not even ma nor pa, of course she would reply by a goo-oo-oo; at any rate, she looks as if she would like to pull her kind sister's face down to kiss it, if she only knew how.

HERE is another kind of baby—a little lamb.
I can't help thinking this lamb has been a little
bit naughty, and has been straying away from its
mother, dancing and frisking about with ever so
many other lambkins at the other side of the
meadow. "How do you know that?" somebody
may ask me. Well, I can see that Mrs. Mother
Sheep looks a little stern, and cross, and anxious;
but now that her lamb has come back to gladden
her old nose—for I suppose you know Mother
Sheep knows her lamb by smelling it, not by
seeing it—she doesn't intend to say very much
about it, after having given a very loud baa-a-aa.

" I'LL tell you a secret." That is what this little girl's mamma is whispering to her. The secret is, that if she will try to be a very good girl, she shall be taken out with her in the afternoon.

HERE is a poor blind man, and his dog Toby.
He has to stand here all day, asking alms of the
passers-by, because he cannot work. He does
not like to be shut up in a work-house, because
he was once a sailor, and served his country
faithfully; so spare him a copper, please.

HERE are some very jolly-looking sailors. They are on their homeward voyage, and are bringing a gay bird of paradise. They seem to be very fond of it, and pleased that it has become so tame.

OH! isn't this comical?   Here is a long, thin
fellow, who is so annoyed because he is so much
taller than his friends, that he goes to Dr. Black
to see if he can give him anything to fill up his
very long legs, and make him grow shorter.   "Oh
yes," says Dr. Black, putting his hands behind his
back; and he calls in his assistant to ask what he
thinks upon the subject.   His opinion is, that the
fellow is ridiculously too long; and he at once
pulls out a pair of scissors, and begins to snip
off a piece of his legs!   Just look at the tall
fellow's face ; see how he is going to roar out !

HERE is a picture of a fine ship on its way home round Cape Horn. It is a very cold part of the sea, and ships often pass great icebergs floating about, and the sailors are very much afraid of them. The birds you see flying about are the great albatrosses. When their wings are spread out, they measure fourteen feet sometimes. You may see the width by measuring that out on the nursery floor.

A VERY merry fellow is this; and such a pretty picture altogether! This little shepherd-boy comes out in the morning, carrying his long crook, and with his bottle of milk slung round his waist. He carries his breakfast and dinner in his wallet on his back; and, followed by his good, clever dog, away he goes to look after his master's flocks. When he has got them all gathered together, he takes out his little flageolet and plays a tune. His dog lies down at his feet to listen; for he is almost as fond of music as his master.

WHO is this fierce-looking man? A New Zealander. He has got all sorts of strange patterns traced out on his skin; that is, he is tattooed. He has tried to make himself as ugly as possible; but he thinks himself very beautiful. New Zealanders used to be cannibals; but they are not so now. Many of them are Christians; and some of them keep the Sabbath even more strictly than we do in some parts of Great Britain, putting away their pretty flaxen mats and bags, and all their week-day work, till the Monday.

HERE is a picture of a scene in Jamaica. These two black fellows have been out in the woods, and they suddenly see a snake wrigging itself away through the thick bushes. One has got such a fright, that he has dropped his axe; but the other is springing forward to kill it before it bite.

OH dear, look here! Ha! ha! ha! Old Mother Hubbard must have forgiven her naughty dog for spoiling her spinning-wheel. We know what a cunning fellow he is, and we are not at all surprised that he has got the good old dame to dance a polka with him before she goes to bed.

HERE is a very different kind of picture, and one that almost makes us shudder. We can hardly believe that there are men who can trust themselves to cross from one side of a ravine to the other by such a slender-looking rope. How sore their hands and feet must be! and how glad they must be when they get to the other side in safety! It is a good thing there are such hardy, brave men in the world; for it helps to make it move on more smoothly.

An English hay-field! See how busy the reapers are mowing down the sweet hay. I hope the little boy under the tree has been helping, and that he is resting after his labours rather than being lazy. It is so nice to toss up the hay when it is dry,—its smell is so sweet.

HERE is a busy group, at any rate. See what a lot of nice sticks they have been gathering in the wood. They are too poor to buy coals, so they go out and gather the broken branches. The farmer does not object to them taking them, because he knows such thrifty, diligent people never destroy the trees; and he often tells the forester to order the workmen to leave as many of the small branches as possible. In this time of dear coals, and dear provisions of every kind, I hope you remember the poor. I know of an old woman in London, who comes twice a week for the old tea-leaves a little boy saves for her.

THIS must be a garden in France, I think. The people there are very fond of the open air, and sometimes take their food in the tea-gardens. They are certainly very merry; but I rather think we, who are accustomed to home comforts, would soon get tired of this noisy out-of-door life. The climate there is so much warmer than ours, that it must be pleasant to have such a nice garden to go to; and the children cannot but enjoy it much.

I THINK these must be very nice children, because
of one thing,—their dog seems to be very fond of
them.   He has come back from a good scamper,
and is looking up in their faces, sure of being
praised.

HERE is a very funny picture. This monkey has found his way into the drawing-room, where sits one of his mistress's visitors. She is rather afraid of him, but thinks it is wiser to keep on friendly terms with him, and is offering him some sweet cake she intended to give to the children. Mr. Monkey, who wants to be thought like his master rather than like a little child, is shaking his head and making all sorts of queer faces and sounds in his throat. It is no wonder the poor visitor is somewhat alarmed.

OH dear, what a sad scene is here! A vessel in distress, with her crew clinging to the sides of the deck. If she is wrecked, I hope they will get off in time in their boats, with a good compass and plenty of food and water to serve till they reach some safe haven, or some land. What dark clouds, and what an angry sea! It is no wonder people are fond of sailors, and like to see them walking about the streets. When we think of the dangers they have to endure, they must enjoy getting back to land again, especially to their own homes, where their wives and children are ready to give them, oh how hearty a welcome!

WHAT is the matter? is anybody killed? I
rather fear this stupid fellow has fired off his gun
in fun and has wounded somebody. His little
brother has fainted with fright.

HERE is a young lady going a long journey. She is sitting on her trunk watching the busy crowds of people coming and going. Everything is so new and strange to her, that she has no time to feel sad.

How busy old Tim is in the threshing-floor! Only
look how his flail is swinging over his head.
Ah, how cunning the ducks are! They have left
the pond, and have gathered round the door, ready
to pick up any stray grains of corn that Tim may
send out. The hens, too, have perched themselves
on the ledge, and are keeping a sharp look-out.

HERE is poor little Johnnie Green crying on his
door-step.   But why is he crying, you would
like to know.   Well, because a naughty boy who
was passing, snatched off his cap and tossed it
somewhere out of Johnnie's reach.   It is well
that his big brother is close at hand to get it for
him, after he hears the cause of his tears.

"MOVE on! move on!"   That is what the police-
man is saying to this strange-looking man.   He
is blind ; but I fear he is only pretending, and is
not such an honest man as the old sailor with the
wooden leg I showed you before.   His dog, too,
looks rather sly ; though, poor beast, it is trying
to do its duty to its master, and is holding out
the tin dish very carefully.   The man is roaring
so loud, that he is frightening the ladies who are
passing ; so no wonder he is told to move on.

THIS is a canoe belonging to the Friendly Islands, in the South Pacific Ocean. When you are old enough, you will be able to read all about them, and how Captain Cook thought this would be a good name for them, because the natives all seemed to live on such friendly terms with one another, and from their politeness to strangers. They live upon cocoa-nuts, yams, hogs, fowls, fish, and shell-fish. They are very fond of bathing themselves in ponds; and even though stagnant, they prefer them to the water of the sea.

" PRETTY cockatoo." The little girls like to pay
him a visit, for he is such a very funny bird. He
is pure white, with such a lovely yellow crest ; and
when he is pleased, he makes it stand up on his
head till you can see every feather quite distinctly.
Unfortunately, when he does that he almost always
gives a terribly loud screech, which forces you to
put your hands to your ears to shut out the ugly
sound. When he gets a piece of sugar, or a bit
of the yolk of an egg, he is so pleased, and makes
a sound like giving you a kiss, to show his thanks.
I hope the little girl who is holding up her finger
is not teazing him, because he may lose his temper
in a moment, and give her a severe bite.

REALLY, Miss Mary, this is a very strange way to use your doll, holding her up by her poor hand, and letting her curls almost sweep the floor. Miss Mary is in a cross humour, and so she is cross with her doll; which is very stupid of her, I am sure you will say. You take very great care of your doll, I am certain; and put her to bed every night, folding up her clothes as you do your own, and teaching her to be a very tidy, well-behaved doll. And you call her by a pretty name, don't you?

I KNOW you will like to see this picture. Isn't
this a dear little pet of a squirrel? He has
come down from the trees to enjoy the warmth
of the sun before it sets, and is eating his supper
with much content. All day he has been very
busy laying up a store of acorns in a hollow of
a tree; for God has taught him to know that
winter, dreary winter, is coming, and that he
must be active in the autumn, else he will starve
when the snow comes.

THIS is a picture of a nautilus; and I am sure papa will be delighted to tell you about this strange creature.　We can

"Learn of the little nautilus to sail,
　Spread the thin oar, or catch the driving gale."

"This is the ship of pearl, which poets feign
　　Sails the unshaded main—
　　The venturous bark that flings
　On the sweet summer wind its purpled wings"

Ah, here is a sad sight. This is a cabin where the slaves live, on a cotton plantation. I am glad to say there are no slaves in America now; and the overseer dare not use that great long whip to force them to work, as he did only a very few years ago. These men have been sent to tie up and whip one of the women, because she did not do as much work as the overseer thought she ought to have done. How glad the negroes must be now to think they cannot be whipped, or sold away from their children and homes; and that they can sing, " No more auction block for me."

THIS is an island in the South Pacific, called Tahiti. The canoes seem to be very different from those of the Friendly Islands; but the people are very different. They used to be in manners quite savages; but the missionaries have done them a great deal of good, and they are becoming just like people in this country. All sorts of roots and plants grow here, and fragrant sandal-wood.

THIS is the picture of the interior of a saloon of one of the steamers to Dublin. It has just newly started, and the passengers are beginning to feel uncomfortable, at least some of them are. The stout old lady is too angry with the gentleman opposite her to think of anything, and scarcely feels the motion of the vessel. She thinks he is very rude because he keeps staring at her grand-daughter, who is so sad about leaving her mamma and papa, that she can think of nothing else. And though she promised to make ever so many sketches, she lets her portfolio lie idly in her lap.

"OH, shocking!" Gertrude is quite right to
say so to this cruel boy, for taking away the
bird's nest. He likes Gertrude, and intended to
make her a present of it; but when he sees how
sorry she is, it is to be hoped he will put it safely
back in the bush again.

HERE is a picture of an English squire walking in his garden. He is very fond of flowers, and keeps a gardener to look after them. Tom the gardener is as proud of the garden as his master is, and always does his best to attend to the flowers. He tenderly carries some of the delicate ones into the green-house the moment the sun sets, lest they should get chilled and die.

"REALLY, did ever any one wear such a funny
bonnet as this young lady?"   Oh yes; not many
years ago, either; and very comfortable it was,
too, I do assure you.   I think the gentleman is
her father, and is an officer; and she is very proud
of walking out with him.   He has taught her to
walk very neatly, and so she is pointing out her
toe as prettily as she can.   Her father is a very
polite man, and is carrying her bag, and even her
parasol, which is rather a comical one.

Now, here is such a very pretty picture that I must tell you a story about it. This is Julia Mayton, the squire's little daughter. She sometimes tires of being in the garden, though she likes the pretty flowers, and is allowed to wander by herself through the wood out to the edge of the common where the shepherd has his sheep feeding. The moment she appears, Help, the shepherd's dog, bounds off to greet her. He likes to be patted by her; and to show that it is only for affection he comes, he always refuses to take any cake or bits of biscuit. He keeps a sharp look-out, too, upon the flock, and if he sees one straying he bounds away back to his duty.

HERE are two sisters sitting on one of the garden
seats.   The younger has brought out her new
book of history her kind grandpapa gave her for
a Christmas present; but she has quite startled
her elder sister by saying that she really does
not like to read it.   She calls it a stupid book.

THIS is a female dancer of Tahiti; and a very funny figure she has made of herself. The things like fans at her back must be intended for wings, I think, and will add much to her grace when she dances. She seems to have no shoes on her feet; but she has been careful to provide herself with a very fine head-dress. You must read all about this beautiful island when you grow bigger, and about its brave inhabitants. You will be very much amused, too, to hear about the strange pillow they lay their heads on when they go to sleep.

"Oh, what a sleepy-headed mamma!"   Ah, but
baby is getting two new teeth, and they have
been so troublesome during the night that poor
mamma did not get a wink of sleep; and now that
they have shot their little white points through
the gums, poor baby is so relieved that he has
popped off to sleep; and his mamma has followed
his example, and dropped off too.   You must be
very careful not to make any noise, in case you
awake them.   Slip about on tip-toe, and shut the
doors very quietly.

HERE is an old man teaching his son to read.
In those days there were no printed books;—all
were written; and so books were very scarce.
Gentlemen used to send their sons to be educated
by the monks. They used to have the most books.
Nearly all the copies of the Bible were in their
keeping. There was a copy chained to a pillar in
old St. Paul's Church in London.

Ah, what is this now? Two anglers busy at work. I greatly fear some foolish trout must have spied out the glittering fly at the end of the line, and swallowed it. Of course he does his best to make his escape, and darts under the bank; but the fisher is trying to force him to come out. He must do so, because the hook is sticking in his poor throat, and he can't bear the pain any longer. It is such a pity he was so greedy, else he might have swam about the pleasant river.

HERE is a poulterer going round selling his fine turkeys and chickens. He is trying to get the doctor of the small town to buy one; but the doctor is telling him that the last was much too dear, and not at all good. Both the men seem surprised; but, of course, the doctor ought to know best.

How would you like to live up on the top of that
high rock ?   The castle is quite a ruin now, and
the ferryman's daughter takes many people in her
boat to see it.   She rows the boat about the lake
all the day, and never seems weary.

I REALLY think this is Old Mother Hubbard's dog again. You remember when she went out to the clothier's to buy him a coat, when she returned home to her own house he was riding on the back of her goat. It is just as well he has the sense to hold on by her horns, for Mrs. Nanny does not seem to be very well pleased, and I can't help thinking that she will toss him off the first moment she can.

THIS is really a very elegant lady; and what a lovely house she seems to live in! I wonder what she is thinking about. She looks rather grave, doesn't she? And this surprises us, because we often think that people who live in grand houses, and wear fine clothes, ought never to be anything but happy. But when we grow older, we find that even the very richest people are sad sometimes, and that they are tempted to envy the happy, contented life of some poor people.

THIS is a very rich little girl. Her father could buy her everything she could desire; but she is very delicate, and all his money cannot purchase health. She has to lie in bed almost all the day; but she has a kind little friend, the rector's daughter, who comes very often and sits beside her and reads to her. Though this little girl cannot run about, she has learned to be content.

HERE is Arthur Young. He is leaving home for
the first time in his life, and is going away to be
a sailor on board a very large ship. He was so
proud of his fine clothes when they came home, and
was never tired of talking about the ship to his
little brothers and sisters; but now he cannot
help thinking that he will not see his dear, kind
mother, for ever so long, and he is trying to listen
very attentively to her last words of advice.

HERE is another view of an island in the Pacific
Ocean.   It is called Raiatea.   Do you notice what
a number of strange-looking trees grow here?   It
would be very nice to be able to get fresh cocoa-nuts
off the trees, and drink the sweet milk for breakfast.
And then it would be delightful to paddle about
in that canoe, and look through the clear water,
down to the very bottom, and watch the lovely
fishes swimming about, blue and yellow, and with
crimson spots sometimes.   How we should laugh,
too, at the funny coloured crabs.

HERE is a picture nearer home.   These children
have a half holiday, and are spending it in the
woods.   They have not forgotten to take their
baby brothers and sisters with them ; and as the
little ones are tired, they are· taking a rest.
Henry wishes his sister Alice to blow very hard
upon the white feathery head of the dandelion
seed, to see if their mother requires her at home ;
but Alice is a little afraid, in case it should be
true, and this makes them all laugh very much.

HEYDAY, and what's the matter here? I fear somebody has been naughty; and even though the
governess is talking kindly, I fear somebody is in
the sulks. Just look at them! I think they
must have been quarrelling, and are both to blame.
It is a great pity they are not friends, because it
is so painful to quarrel with one's playmates;
it makes everything feel wrong together. I do
hope they will forgive each other.

GATHERING pretty posies.   Oh, do look at the
dove taking a peep at her! and the squirrels know
they need not scamper off, for she is too good to
hurt them.

WHO is this diligent little girl, I wonder? See
how she is polishing the table! This is little
Mary Tom, the gardener's daughter; and, as her
mother is helping in the garden, she is keeping
house with her sister Jane. Jane is just setting
out to the village to buy something nice for her
father's tea; and she is telling Mary to be careful,
and not scrub the paint off,—as if Mary would be
so foolish!

(446) 8

"FIRE! fire!"   How could the old school-master
expect to get his pupils to come to their lessons
after hearing that cry! Why, just look! there's old
Nanny, who keeps the apple-stall at the corner,
looking quite bewildered, and asking the boys to
tell her what is the matter. Instead of being angry,
I think the school-master had better put on his hat
and set off too after his pupils;—what do you think?

"HOLD hard! hold hard!" Don't you see Tom
and Dick have gone down, and Harry is about to
follow? Who would mind a tumble on such
lovely ice? Oh, look there!—a gentleman has lost
his balance, and he is going after his hat, I fear,
crash down on the ice. It will be worse for him
than for the boys.

WHAT is this you are looking at so earnestly,
Miss Eliza? Ah, yes, the figure under the glass
shade. You do well to look at it. It is very
pretty indeed. Only be careful. Don't let it
slip from the table. See how near it is to the
edge.

TRAPPERS out hunting. This is in the far west of North America, and it is a very cold place. It is a pity the snow is so deep that it has covered the hunters' feet; for you would have got a surprise had you seen their snow-shoes, which are very curious and very large.

HERE is a kind old grandmamma taking a pleasant
stroll out in the woods.   The girls have been
filling their baskets with wild-flowers, and the
boys have been playing at hounds and hares.
They are now going to rest, and listen to some of
grandmamma's old stories.

HERE is a little boy setting out on his apprentice-
ship.   His dog wants to go with him, but he is
obliged to tell him that he must not go any further.
The dog, which has been his faithful companion,
is not able to understand that, though he is a
clever dog.   But he knows that there is something wrong, and at last he hears the words, " Go
home, sir."

YES, and we too must part, my dear.   And here is Old Mother Hubbard for the last picture in my Scrap-Book; and for me she is making her very best courtesy for your patience; and the dog is making his most elegant bow, though I wish he had not been so rude as to turn his back when saying to you "Farewell."

www.ingramcontent.com/pod-product-compliance
Lightning Source LLC
Chambersburg PA
CBHW022140020726
47496CB00008B/2491